Transformers: Hunt for the Decepticons: Training Day
HASBRO and its logo, TRANSFORMERS and all related characters are trademarks of Hasbro and are used with permission. © 2011 Hasbro. All Rights Reserved. © 2011 DreamWorks, LLC and Paramount Pictures Corporation. All Rights Reserved. Manufactured in China. No part of this book may be used or reproduced in any manner whatsoever without written permission except in the case of brief quotations embodied in critical articles and reviews. For information address HarperCollins Children's Books, a division of HarperCollins Publishers, 10 East 53rd Street, New York, NY 10022.
www.icanread.com

Library of Congress catalog card number: 2010922247
ISBN 978-0-06-199177-6
Typography by John Sazaklis

11 12 13 14 15   SCP   10 9 8 7 6 5 4 3 2 1   ❖   First Edition

Dear Parent:
Your child's love of reading starts here!

Every child learns to read in a different way and at his or her own speed. Some go back and forth between reading levels and read favorite books again and again. Others read through each level in order. You can help your young reader improve and become more confident by encouraging his or her own interests and abilities. From books your child reads with you to the first books he or she reads alone, there are I Can Read Books for every stage of reading:

SHARED READING
Basic language, word repetition, and whimsical illustrations, ideal for sharing with your emergent reader

BEGINNING READING
Short sentences, familiar words, and simple concepts for children eager to read on their own

READING WITH HELP
Engaging stories, longer sentences, and language play for developing readers

READING ALONE
Complex plots, challenging vocabulary, and high-interest topics for the independent reader

ADVANCED READING
Short paragraphs, chapters, and exciting themes for the perfect bridge to chapter books

I Can Read Books have introduced children to the joy of reading since 1957. Featuring award-winning authors and illustrators and a fabulous cast of beloved characters, I Can Read Books set the standard for beginning readers.

A lifetime of discovery begins with the magical words **"I Can Read!"**

Visit www.icanread.com for information
on enriching your child's reading experience.

I Can Read!

READING 2 WITH HELP

TRANS FORMERS

Training Day

HUNT for the DECEPTICONS
TRANSFORMERS.COM

Adapted by Michael Teitelbaum
Illustrated by MADA Design, Inc.

HARPER
An Imprint of HarperCollinsPublishers

A black 4x4 pickup truck
rumbled to a stop in the desert.
A sleek silver Corvette
and a slick yellow Camaro
screeched to a stop,
throwing up a spray of sand.

Then a blue semitruck dropped
from the sky.
These vehicles were all Transformers.
They were Autobots,
sworn to stop the evil Decepticons.

"Autobots, roll out!"
shouted Optimus Prime,
the leader of the Autobots.
Ironhide switched
into his robot form.

Sideswipe stood up
on his rear wheels.

His wheels changed into arms and legs.

His hood and grill turned into a head.

When he was finished,

Sideswipe was a robot.

Bumblebee began
to switch modes.
Headlights, fenders, wheels, and doors
all changed into arms, legs,
a head, and a body.
Bumblebee stood tall.

Finally, Optimus Prime changed.

"The Decepticon threat has risen again,"

the Autobot leader said.

"I have called you here

so we can train

for the upcoming battle."

Sideswipe and Bumblebee
changed back into their vehicle forms.
"Hey, Bumblebee, I'll race you
to that mountain!
That'll be good training," said Sideswipe.

"You're on!" Bumblebee responded using his car radio. Sideswipe and Bumblebee zoomed off across the desert. They saw a village at the bottom of a mountain.

4NZ Z454

What the Autobots did not know
was that beneath that very mountain,
evil was hard at work.
Megatron, leader of the Decepticons,
and Starscream were digging
lots of underground tunnels.

"Once these tunnels are complete, we will be able to move freely, unseen by the Autobots," said Megatron. "We can surprise them in the coming battle."

Meanwhile, back outside,
a giant boulder suddenly started
rolling down the mountain.
"That boulder is going to crush
the entire village!" Sideswipe cried.

"Change!" Bumblebee radioed.
Then he and Sideswipe switched
into their robot forms.
"We've got to stop that boulder!"
Sideswipe cried.

Bumblebee's right arm changed
into a plasma cannon.
He fired a blast at the boulder.
The huge rock broke
into many smaller pieces.

Sideswipe extended his swords.

He sliced the smaller rocks

into harmless pebbles.

"The village is safe now!" Sideswipe said.

"Let's keep training for the

Decepticon attack."

Meanwhile, Optimus Prime
and Ironhide traveled to a forest.
There, they bounced along a path
through the woods.
"I'm built for this off-road stuff,"
said Ironhide in his 4x4 form.
"But you're not."

"I must be ready to battle
the Decepticons wherever they appear,"
Optimus Prime said.
"That is why we are training."

Rolling out of the woods,
the two Autobots came to a dam.
They rumbled along the road
leading over the top.
Suddenly, the dam burst.

Water poured through a huge hole.

"This whole area will be flooded!"

Ironhide cried.

"Switch to robot mode and follow me,"

Optimus Prime said.

The two Autobots changed
into their robot forms.
They ran alongside the raging water.
"My scanner shows me
that there is a rock quarry ahead,"
Ironhide said.
"Hurry!"
"Quickly, pile up these rocks,"
said Optimus Prime.
"They can help hold back the water."
Working swiftly,
Ironhide and Optimus Prime
stacked up the giant rocks.

Using all their strength, the two Autobots
finished piling up the rocks.
The water slowed to a trickle.
"This should hold until the dam
can be rebuilt," said Optimus Prime.

Back in the desert, Sideswipe and
Bumblebee continued their race.
Suddenly, the earth began to shake.
The ground between them split open.
"Earthquake! Better call Optimus Prime!"

Bumblebee signaled Optimus Prime.

In a flash, the Autobot leader

and Ironhide sped back to the desert.

The desert continued to shake.

The crack in the ground grew wider.

The two Autobot teams
stood on either side of the crack.
"Why are all these natural disasters
happening now?"
Optimus Prime wondered.

Without warning, two Decepticons
burst from the crack in the ground.
"Megatron and Starscream!"
cried Optimus Prime.

"So these were no natural disasters!"
Optimus Prime said.
"You caused them!"
"And now we will cause
the destruction of the Autobots!"
Megatron shouted.

"Autobots, prepare for battle!"
Optimus Prime shouted.
The fight was on.
Bumblebee fired his plasma cannon.
Sideswipe extended his swords.
The two Autobots battled Starscream.

Optimus Prime and Ironhide
fought Megatron.
"You cannot win, Megatron!"
shouted Optimus Prime.
"We have been training
and are prepared for this battle."

All the Autobots' hard work paid off.

Megatron and Starscream retreated.

"We will fight another day, Prime!"

Megatron shouted.

"And we will be ready!"

said Optimus Prime.